W9-ARU-738

INTRODUCTION

The American Buffalo are native to Yellowstone
   Park.
The Buffalo appear docile or friendly; however,
Buffalo do not like people or other animals to come
   too close. They like their space.

I AM AN ARO PUBLISHING 40 WORD BOOK

MY 40 WORDS ARE:

A	moose
and	my
are	need
Buffa	needs
buffalo	no
but	near
deer	one
else	place
ever	private
elk	quiet
fill	said
go	space
get	still
here	too
I	they
it	this
is	there
like	where
lonely	will
many	when

ISBN 0-89868-175-8 — Library Bound
ISBN 0-89868-176-6 — Soft Bound

YELLOWSTONE CRITTERS

BUFFA BUFFALO

BY BOB REESE

ARO PUBLISHING

"I need a place," said Buffalo,

"where no one else will ever go.

Too many elk, moose, and deer,

fill my space when they get near.

A buffalo needs a private place."

A buffalo needs a private space.

"I need a place," said Buffalo,

"where no one else will ever go.

There are too many elk.

There are too many deer.

There are too many moose.

But, there is no one here!"

"I like this place," said Buffalo,

"where no one else will ever go."

"It is quiet here," said Buffalo,

"where no one else will ever go."

"It is lonely here," said Buffalo,

"where no one else will ever go.

**They fill my space
when they get near;**

**but, I still like elk,
moose and deer.''**